FRANKiE SPARKS

AND THE TALENT SHOW TRICK

ALSO BY
MEGAN FRAZER BLAKEMORE

Frankie Sparks and the Class Pet

FRANKIE SPARKS, THIRD-GRADE INVENTOR

FRANKIE SPARKS

AND THE TALENT SHOW TRICK

BOOK 2

BY MEGAN FRAZER BLAKEMORE

ILLUSTRATED BY NADJA SARELL

ALADDIN   NEW YORK LONDON TORONTO SYDNEY NEW DELHI

This book is a work of fiction. Any references to historical events, real people, or real places are used fictitiously. Other names, characters, places, and events are products of the author's imagination, and any resemblance to actual events or places or persons, living or dead, is entirely coincidental.

❦ ALADDIN
An imprint of Simon & Schuster Children's Publishing Division
1230 Avenue of the Americas, New York, New York 10020
First Aladdin paperback edition June 2019
Text copyright © 2019 by Megan Frazer Blakemore
Illustrations copyright © 2019 by Nadja Sarell
Also available in an Aladdin hardcover edition.
All rights reserved, including the right of reproduction in whole or in part in any form.
ALADDIN and related logo are registered trademarks of Simon & Schuster, Inc.
For information about special discounts for bulk purchases, please contact Simon & Schuster Special Sales at 1-866-506-1949 or business@simonandschuster.com.
The Simon & Schuster Speakers Bureau can bring authors to your live event. For more information or to book an event contact the Simon & Schuster Speakers Bureau at 1-866-248-3049 or visit our website at www.simonspeakers.com.
Series art directed by Laura Lyn DiSiena
Interior designed by Tiara Iandiorio
The illustrations for this book were rendered in pencil line on paper and digital flat tones.
The text of this book was set in Nunito.
Manufactured in the United States of America 0519 OFF
10 9 8 7 6 5 4 3 2 1
Library of Congress Control Number 2018958109
ISBN 978-1-5344-3047-1 (hc)
ISBN 978-1-5344-3046-4 (pbk)
ISBN 978-1-5344-3048-8 (eBook)

Dedicated to my South Portland
librarian friends, who inspire
kids like Frankie every day

CONTENTS

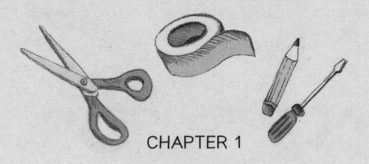

CHAPTER 1

Magician

FRANKIE SPARKS SAT IN THE FRONT row of the town theater, her hands cradled in her lap. Next to her was her best friend, Maya. They both stared into the swirling purple mist on the stage.

Crash! Maya jumped, but Frankie leaned in to see better.

Flash! A blinding light, and then, stepping from the cloud, a tall woman with brown skin and curls just like Frankie's walked to the center of the stage.

"I am the great Tatiana Celestia," she announced. "Prepare to be amazed."

Frankie was prepared!

Frankie was, hands down, the world's greatest third-grade inventor, but that wasn't the only thing she was interested in. When Mr. Winklesmith, the owner of Wink's Magic and Games Emporium, had told her that Tatiana Celestia, one of the world's greatest magicians, was going to be in town, Frankie had been beyond excited. She had checked out all the magic books in the library, even the ones with really big words, and made her way through them.

Now she watched, wide-eyed, as Tatiana

pulled a trombone out of her billowy sleeve. The magician held her lips up to the mouthpiece and blew.

Nothing.

Tatiana frowned and shook the horn. She blew again.

Still nothing.

Then she pointed right at Frankie and asked, "Can you give me a hand?"

Frankie leaped to her feet and climbed onto the stage. There were few things Frankie liked better than being onstage. The crowd clapped politely.

Tatiana said, "This is my grandma's trombone. She used to tour around with a big swing band. Once, she even played with Ella Fitzgerald."

Frankie knew who Ella Fitzgerald was: a jazz singer who happened to be Frankie's grandmother's favorite. "Really?" she asked.

"Really," Tatiana said with a smile. "So this horn is pretty old." She shook a scarf from her sleeve. "Can you give it a good wipe-down?"

Frankie did as she was asked, carefully polishing the horn and the long brass tube. A trombone was a funny-looking invention, and Frankie began wondering how it worked.

"Yes, my grandma played trombone, and my mama was a dancer, toured the whole world. I'm following in their footsteps." Tatiana turned to Frankie. "That looks good, my friend."

Frankie handed the horn back to Tatiana, who held it to her lips once more. She began to play. A low, beautiful note rang out. And, as

if riding on the note, bubbles streamed out of the horn.

The crowd gasped, and kids reached up to pop the bubbles.

Tatiana kept playing and did a little dance. She stomped her feet to make a beat. Frankie joined in by clapping. She could see Tatiana smiling as she played the horn. When the song was finished, Tatiana lowered her horn. "Thank you, friend," she said to Frankie, then turned to the audience. "Let's give this young lady a round of applause." As Frankie returned to her seat, the crowd clapped enthusiastically.

"That was incredible!" Maya exclaimed.

Frankie agreed, nodding her head. But her brain was already spinning a mile a minute. She had a new idol, and she was hatching a new plan.

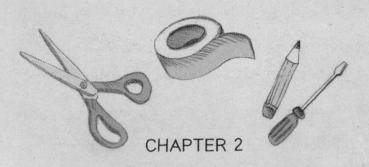

CHAPTER 2

Magic Duo

AFTER THE MAGIC SHOW, MAYA AND Frankie had gone backstage and met Tatiana. Frankie had told her how impressed she was, and then asked, "How do you become a magician?"

"Same way you do anything else," Tatiana had said. "You study and you practice."

That's exactly what Frankie did. With Maya's help, she practiced magic tricks that wowed, zowed, and amazed. Finally Frankie and Maya were ready to perform. Sure, their first show was in Maya's living room, but Frankie felt sure they'd hit the big time any day now.

They did a card trick and a scarf trick, and they were in the middle of their disappearing-Frankie trick when things started to go a little off track.

"Ta-da!" Maya called out. With a flourish, she yanked a bright red sheet off the cardboard box. Just ten seconds before, Frankie had crouched down inside the box. Now she had disappeared! Maya held both hands up in an exaggerated shrug. She looked into the open front of the box. "Where could she be?"

"Someplace where we can't hear her," Maya's older brother, Matt, said. "Which is a nice change, if you ask me."

"Nobody asked you." It was Frankie's voice, coming from behind the box, where she was hiding. Frankie immediately clapped her hand over her mouth. Tatiana never would have ruined a trick by calling out.

Maya, though, was the perfect magician's assistant. She kept going like it was all part of the act. "Where could she be?" Maya asked again. She held her hand up to her forehead and peered around the room. "I can hear her, but she has vanished!"

Matt opened his mouth as if he were going to say something, but Maya's dad gave him a look.

"Frankie?" Maya asked. "Frankie, are you ready to come back from the great wherever?"

Maya's dog, Opus, padded in from the other

room. He saw Frankie and sniffed the air. He knew Frankie often kept treats like goldfish crackers or broken pretzels in her pockets. Frankie shook her head frantically at Opus. "I'm ready!" she said hurriedly.

Maya threw the sheet back over the box. Frankie carefully lifted the hatch she had constructed in the box and climbed inside. Frankie made all her own magic tricks. Mr. Winklesmith had told her about magic cabinets, and she had designed and made her own cabinet out of cardboard boxes. The cabinet had a false back that she could crawl out of. It looked like a real cupboard, and she was even able to have a vase with fake flowers.

Opus gave a whimper and tried to follow her through the hatch. "Shoo!" she called out.

But by then his head was stuck. So Frankie grabbed him around the waist and tugged him into the box with her. Once they were both inside, Frankie said, "Abracadabra, bring me back to this terrestrial plain!"

Maya pulled the sheet away again, and there were Frankie and Opus, both grinning wildly. "Ta-da!" Maya called. She helped Frankie to her feet, and together they bowed. Opus barked, and the audience, except for Matt, clapped.

It wasn't a huge audience—just Frankie's parents, her aunt Gina, Maya's parents, and Matt—but Frankie slurped up the applause just the same. She loved the hoots and the claps. She squeezed Maya's hand, and Maya squeezed back.

"Bravo!" Frankie's mom called, standing up. She was clapping like crazy, and Frankie knew she thought that was the end of the show.

"Wait!" Frankie said. "We have one last trick. And for this we need a volunteer named Matt."

Matt scowled, but Frankie was pretty sure he was secretly pleased. He came up onto their stage—it was really just a blanket on the floor—and brushed the hair out of his eyes. "What do I have to do?"

Frankie tied a blindfold over her eyes while Maya took a deck of cards out of Frankie's magic bag. "Shuffle the deck and then pick a card, any card," Maya said.

Matt shuffled. Then he shuffled some more. And some more.

"Matt!" Maya cried. "Just pick a card already!"

"I don't want you to cheat me by setting up the cards ahead of time," Matt replied.

Frankie smirked. Magic tricks weren't cheats. They used illusions and the art of misdirection.

Finally, Matt chose a card.

"Show it to the audience," Maya instructed. "Now place it back in the deck." She split the deck in two so that Matt could put his card back in. Frankie untied her blindfold. Timing was everything here. Maya waited just a second after Frankie had the blindfold off, long enough for Frankie to see the bottom card in the top half of the deck. It was the two of hearts. Then Maya put the deck back together and handed it to Frankie.

"As you saw, I have not touched this deck

in the whole process," Frankie said. "Matt had a chance to shuffle. Then he took his card, and then my assistant gave the cards to me. No cheats." She held the deck in her hand and closed her eyes tightly. This trick was all about the dramatics, which she loved. "Hmm. A vision is coming to me." She opened her eyes and started flipping cards over one at a time. Sometimes she paused. "Maybe," she began. Then shook her head. "No, not this one." Matt smirked. Frankie kept going. Then Frankie flipped over the two of hearts. She nodded and flipped over the next card. The jack of diamonds. She hesitated. She closed her eyes again, then suddenly opened them wide. "This one!" she cried. "This is your card!"

Matt's mouth opened in surprise. Opus,

catching the excitement, barked. Frankie put her magician's hat on and curtsied.

"Thank you for your participation, sir. You may take your seat," Maya told him.

"And that concludes our show." Frankie flipped off her magic hat, and a bouquet of silk flowers popped out.

The grown-ups, and even Matt, clapped their hearts out while Frankie and Maya beamed.

"How did you do that?" Matt asked.

Maya giggled. "You know that a magician never reveals her tricks."

"Only to her best friend and spectacular assistant," Frankie said. "That was a good trick. But I think the kids at school are going to like the one where I make the coin come out of Maya's nose the best."

"The kids at school?" Maya asked.

"Sure!" Frankie said. "We're in third grade now, so we can be in the talent show. Ms. Cupid made the announcement about it this morning." Frankie zipped up her magic bag, which was one of her mom's old briefcases painted with glitter glue.

"The talent show?" Maya asked.

Frankie nodded. "Tryouts are on Monday. We are definitely ready!"

Opus sat down right at Frankie's feet.

"I think it's a great idea," Maya's dad said. "The two of you are a magical duo. A pair of aces."

"More like the gruesome twosome," Matt teased.

"Anyway," Maya's dad said, "I think it will

be great for you both to get up onstage. Especially you, Maya."

"Me too," Frankie's mom agreed. "But no more practicing tonight. The only magic I want to see is you going to bed without a fuss." She handed Frankie her coat, which Frankie shrugged on.

"I already signed us up," Frankie said. "Our audition is at three thirty in the gym."

"I can get the girls after their tryout," Frankie's mom offered.

"See," Frankie said. "Easy-peasy."

"Lemon squeezy," Maya replied.

Frankie and her parents stepped out into the cold night air. They said good night to Aunt Gina, who got into her car to drive home. The sky was clear, and Frankie could see all the stars in the galaxy, it seemed.

She thought about Tatiana Celestia. Frankie wondered if Tatiana had ever done a school talent show.

In a lot of ways, magic was like inventing. There was a lot of science behind magic tricks. Magicians often came up with new tricks, and they had to test and retest them, like when inventors designed inventions. Plus, magic was just plain cool.

"Hey, guys?" she asked.

"Yes, Frankie?" her dad replied.

"Do you think I can be a magician *and* an inventor?"

"I would be very surprised if you were not both of those and about six things more," her mom told her.

"It seems like inventing and magic have a lot in common," her dad said.

Frankie nodded. She liked the idea of being not only Frankie Sparks, the world's greatest third-grade inventor, but also Frankie Sparks, third-grade *magician*. She liked it so much that when she got home, she got herself ready for bed without a fuss. She crawled right under her covers, where she read a chapter in one of her magic books and then fell asleep and dreamed about herself onstage.

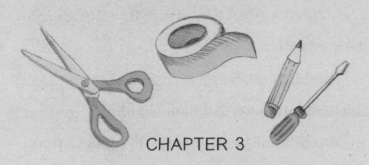

CHAPTER 3

Where's Maya?

"HOW DO YOU MAKE A TISSUE DANCE?" Ravi asked Frankie when she came into the classroom. Normally she liked jokes, but she was looking for Maya. Maya hadn't been out on the playground before school. Frankie told herself not to get nervous, but it's hard not to be nervous when you are a magician and you can't find your assistant. She felt like she had root beer and popcorn dancing in her stomach.

"Come on, Frankie," Ravi said. "How do you make a tissue dance?"

"I don't know, Ravi."

She peered around him. No Maya.

"You put a little boogie in it!" Ravi slapped his leg. "Good one, right?"

"Uh-huh," Frankie said. She shoved her coat into her cubby and started walking toward her desk.

Ravi was right beside her. "Here's another one," he said. "What did the Atlantic Ocean say to the Pacific Ocean?"

"What?" she asked.

"Nothing. It just waved!" Ravi guffawed, but Frankie dropped into her seat.

Where was Maya? The auditions were this afternoon. Frankie's mom had driven her to school so that they could bring in her magic cabinet and put it on the stage. Frankie had worn her abracadabra socks. Her magic bag was in Ms. Cupid's closet. Frankie was all ready to rock the tryout. Except Maya wasn't at school yet. Frankie couldn't do her act without her assistant.

"I'm trying out for the talent show," Ravi said. "With jokes. My mom wanted me to play the piano, but I was like, 'No way. I am a comedian.' I've been practicing all weekend."

"I've been practicing my whole life," Frankie said with a sigh.

"I think that's an exaggeration," Ravi said. He sat down in his seat, which was across from hers. Sometimes Ms. Cupid let Frankie and Maya sit together, but this was not one of those weeks. Frankie's seat did look right across the room at Maya's, though. Normally that was great, because normally Maya was in the seat. But not this morning.

Frankie twisted around to watch the door, so that she would see Maya the second she got to class. There was no sign of her, and then Ms. Flower, the principal, came on the announcements and they stood for the Pledge of Allegiance. As soon as that was finished, they started morning meeting, and of course the share question was about the talent show.

Everyone was trying out! Lila Jones was going to tap-dance. Luke Winslow was going to do basketball-dribbling tricks. Even mopey old William Percival had a talent: yo-yo tricks. When it was Frankie's turn, she looked at the door. "Maya and I are going to do a magic show," Frankie said. Even to her, her voice sounded as flat as a pancake, with none of its usual zest. "I'm the magician, and Maya is my assistant."

"Maya isn't here," Lila said. She smiled at Frankie.

"I know." Frankie's voice wobbled. She actually felt hot tears on her cheeks.

"I'm sure she'll be here soon," Ms. Cupid said. "I don't have a call in from the office that she's absent, so maybe she's just running behind. Maybe she overslept!"

Frankie nodded, but she knew there was no chance of that. Maya was never late. No one in her family ever overslept. Frankie's dad said their internal clocks were always set to the right time.

"Maybe she's sick," Luke said. "Maybe she barfed all night long. That happened to me once. I—"

Ms. Cupid held up both hands. "Red light, Luke. I don't think we need those details." She stood up. "Gather your things. We're going down to meet with our kindergarten buddies."

Frankie groaned. Normally she loved learning-buddies time. Her buddy was a cool kid named Violet. Violet always wore tutus and said she was a unicorn princess from outer space. On reading days, Frankie would bring books about the planets, and they would talk about what it would be like to visit each one.

It was hard for Frankie to get through some of the science words, but Violet didn't mind, and so those days Frankie usually felt like a rock-star supergenius.

But the kindergarten wing was as far from the front door as Frankie could get. She wouldn't be able to watch for Maya.

As they walked in the hall, Lila Jones whispered, "Is Maya really going to do the talent show with you?"

"She is," Frankie whispered back.

"But she isn't here. If you don't audition, you can't be in the show," Lila said.

"I *know*," Frankie snapped back.

"Frankie!" Ms. Cupid said from the front of the line, without even looking back at Frankie to see if it had been her. "I expect a nice quiet line from third graders. We're setting an example for our kindergarten friends." Ms. Cupid stopped at the door of the kindergarten classroom. "Are you ready to set a good example?" Ms. Cupid asked Frankie.

"Yes, Ms. Cupid," Frankie replied. Out of the corner of her eye, Frankie saw Lila smirking. Stupid Lila! She had been the one talking to Frankie in the first place.

Ms. Cupid pushed open the door, and Frankie and the rest of the third graders walked in to meet their kindergarten buddies. It was a learning-games day, and the kindergartners were already waiting with dice, cards, blocks, and more.

"Greetings, Earthling," Violet said to Frankie. "How are you today?"

"Cruddy," Frankie replied.

"What does that mean?"

Frankie sighed. "It means awful. Rainy-Saturday, soggy-cornflakes awful."

"That's really bad."

Frankie nodded. "What's the game we're playing?"

Violet explained the card game, called Top It. There was a card already flipped over, and the first person had to put down a card with a higher number than that one, and the next person had to put down a higher card than *that* one. The person who placed the last card won and got to keep all the cards. Frankie started shuffling.

"Wow!" Violet said. "You're really good at shuffling."

"I have to be," Frankie said. "I'm a magician."

"For real?" Violet asked. Before Frankie could answer, Violet poked the kindergartner next to her. "Andre, my learning buddy is a magician!"

Andre was working with Ravi, who rolled a pair of dice and got double sixes. Andre didn't even notice. "A real magician?"

"Sure," Frankie said with a shrug, trying to act like it was no big deal. But really, being a magician was a *very big deal*!

"You are so lucky!" Andre said. He turned back to Ravi. "Are you a real magician too?"

"I'm a comedian."

Andre looked at him blankly.

"I tell jokes." Ravi pointed at the dice. "Come on, let's play."

"Yeah," Frankie said. "We should play this card game." She dealt ten cards to herself and ten to Violet just like Violet told her to.

"Wait!" Violet said. She jumped up and

got something that looked like two halves of

a paper plate held together with clothespins. Frankie couldn't help but be intrigued. She leaned a little closer and saw that someone had drawn fingers on the plates so that they looked like hands. "It's to hold my cards," Violet explained. "Ten is too many to hold at once, so Ms. Barton made these for us. Anyway, are you going to be in the talent show?"

Frankie took a deep breath. She was *supposed* to be in the talent show. She was supposed to be a star. But without Maya, how could she do it?

Frankie wished she really had magic powers. She would cast a spell to make Maya appear.

"Abracadabra alakazam," Frankie whispered. "Make my friend Maya appear."

The door opened. Frankie looked up.

"Maya!" she cried. She jumped up, ran to Maya, and wrapped her arms around her best friend.

Maya smiled back at her. "Sorry I'm late," she said. "I forgot to tell you I had a dentist appointment this morning."

When Frankie sat back down next to Violet, both Violet and Andre were gaping at her.

"You really *are* a magician," Violet whispered.

"Yep," Frankie said. "And now that my trusty assistant is here, nothing can go wrong!"

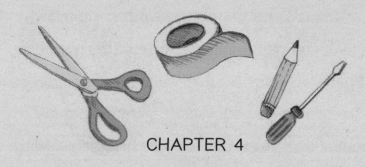

CHAPTER 4

Choke!

FRANKIE'S STOMACH FLIP-FLOPPED OVER and over. She felt like she was riding on the world's most super-duper roller coaster, but her feet were on the floor backstage at school. She had her black magician hat on and her cape. She had her magic bag full of tricks and props. And waiting onstage was her magic cabinet. It was time for the talent show tryouts, and she and Maya were next.

Onstage, Lila finished up her tap dance. Her black shoes shone like the dark coffee Frankie's mom liked to drink. Normally that would have made Frankie's stomach tight with envy—she loved shiny, new shoes—but right now she didn't care. Nothing could ruin this moment for her.

Maya chewed on her fingernails at the edge of the stage. Frankie peeked out to see the rest of the kids sitting on the floor. "There's twenty-seven kids out there," Frankie said. "I counted them all."

Maya gulped.

Lila bowed, and the kids sitting on the gym floor waiting to audition clapped. Frankie clapped too. Maya, though, stood still.

"Frankie! Maya!" Ms. Frost called from the

other side of the stage. Ms. Frost was the first-grade teacher who ran the talent show every year. "You're up!"

Frankie grabbed Maya's hand and pulled her onto the stage. The lights were on in the gym, and there were no spotlights, but that was okay by Frankie. She was up on the stage, and people were watching her. What's more, they were about to be amazed!

"Ladies and gentleman," Frankie called out. "Boys and girls! I am the Great Francesca!" Normally Frankie did not like to be called by her full name, but she thought it sounded more magician-like than "Frankie." "And this is my amazing assistant, Maya the Magnificent!"

Maya didn't move. She stood with her eyes wide, staring out at the crowd.

Frankie turned and looked over her shoulder at Maya. Maya's mouth opened and closed. It looked like she was saying words, but not a sound came out.

"That's a cool trick, Frankie!" Luke called from the audience. "You made Maya's voice disappear!"

Maya snapped her mouth shut.

"Are you okay?" Frankie asked.

"I'm fine," Maya whispered. "Just start."

"For my first trick," Frankie said. "I will make a flower grow out of this plain vase." She pulled a red plastic vase out of her magic bag. "Maya, can you please show the audience that this is a regular, empty vase?"

She handed the vase to Maya. Maya's fingers closed around the vase, but when she held it up, her hand shook so much that the vase slipped from her fingers and clattered onto the floor. A quiet gasp came from the audience.

Maya scooped it up and held it in front of her. She tilted it toward the audience. "As you can see, this is an empty vessel," she croaked. It sounded like the words were being pulled out of her and scraped across the pavement. And the vase shook like someone driving along that bumpy road.

"Hold it still," Frankie whispered as she extended her own hand, which hid a flower on a spring. In order to make the trick work, she had to have her hand right over the top of the vase, but the way the vase was bouncing around, it was impossible. "Maya!"

"I'm trying," Maya said.

Frankie took a deep breath. "Abracadabra, reveal my power—into this vase, put a flower!" She let the flower expand in her hand. The spring was supposed to shoot the stem into the glass, but Maya's jittery hand jerked the vase out of the way, and instead the flower fell to the floor. "Whoops!" Frankie exclaimed.

Ms. Frost clapped, though, and so did

the rest of the audience. Frankie was pretty sure they were just being nice. She knew she should be grateful, but the pity tasted bitter and sour at the same time. She bent over and snatched the flower from the floor. Normally she pulled it out of the vase and tucked it behind Maya's ear, but this time she just tossed it aside.

"For our next trick," Frankie said, "my assistant will begin by putting this silk cloth on the cabinet."

Maya took the cloth from Frankie. She held it tightly in her hands. She lifted it high so that it would fall gently onto the box. But when she let go, it fell with a flop. Maya tried to spread it out, but her hands acted as though she were a robot with a glitch in its code. She pushed and pulled and twisted until the cloth was practically a knot.

"You know what," Frankie said to the audience. "We're just going to skip that trick." She whispered to Maya, "Let's do the card trick. Ask for a volunteer from the audience."

"We would have—I mean, for the next trick we can . . . we need a volunteer. From the audience. An audience volunteer."

Half the group shot their hands up, and then Maya called on Luke, of all people. Sure, the trick had gone well at home with Matt. But this was their tryout, and they were already having trouble. Maya should've chosen someone friendly, like Ravi. Frankie almost called out "Just kidding!" but Luke was already racing up onto the stage. Frankie took the deck of cards out of her bag and placed them on the cabinet. This was Maya's cue, but she didn't say anything.

Frankie cleared her throat.

Maya still didn't say anything.

"Maya," Frankie said. "Please have Luke shuffle and choose a card."

"Why do I have to shuffle?" Luke asked. "You didn't say I had to shuffle."

"*Can* you shuffle?" Frankie asked.

"Sure I can," Luke said, but his cheeks were pink.

"You have to shuffle," Frankie said with a sigh. None of this was going the way she had planned, and now Maya had gone and picked Luke, the one person most likely to make things even worse. "So you know I'm not cheating."

"But if you know I'm going to shuffle, isn't that still cheating?" he asked.

"How could I possibly know how you are going to shuffle?" She glared at him as she reached for her blindfold.

Maya picked up the deck of cards.

"Luke, will you please shuffle and . . ."

Maya's voice petered out as the cards dropped from her hands and drifted down like leaves in fall, all across the stage.

"Maya!" Frankie exclaimed. "What is wrong with you?"

"Fifty-two pickup!" Luke cried. "I love this game."

Without a word, Maya ran offstage, leaving Frankie there surrounded by cards. Luke scrambled around, trying to pick them all up.

"Um," Frankie said. "We seem to be having some—I mean—"

"Can you do it without Maya?" Ms. Frost called from the side of the stage.

Without Maya? How could Ms. Frost even ask such a question? Frankie shook her head hard.

"Well, then, I'm afraid you're going to have to clear the stage."

Frankie's heart fell, just like the cards.

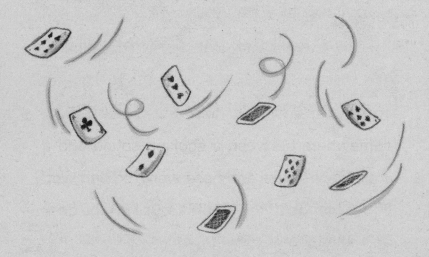

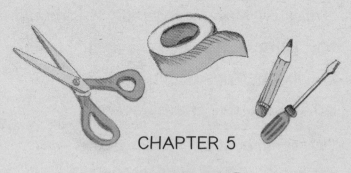

CHAPTER 5

Hiding

IT TOOK FRANKIE ALMOST TEN MINUTES to find Maya. She was in the library, back in the story corner, *under* one of the beanbags. The only reason Frankie was able to find her was because of the noise she was making, somewhere between a choking sound and a wail. Maya's eyes and nose were red and wet. Frankie grabbed the box of tissues off the desk and sat down next to Maya.

"I'm sorry," Maya whispered.

"I'm sorry too," Frankie said. "I shouldn't have yelled at you."

"That's okay."

"What happened?" Frankie asked.

Maya shrugged.

"The first trick went a little rough," Frankie said, "but I think everyone was still excited about seeing some magic. People were clapping—"

"That's the problem," Maya sighed.

"People clapping?"

"People," Maya answered.

She took a tissue and blew hard into it. She made a honking noise that normally would have made both girls burst into laughter, but this time neither of them was smiling.

"All those people," Maya said. "Looking at me."

"That's what an audience does, Maya," Frankie said. "It's not like they can look away." Frankie was working hard to try to understand what Maya was saying. For Frankie, there was nothing better than standing up onstage with an audience watching her. "I mean, when we decided to do the talent show, you had to know there was going to be an audience."

"I *didn't* decide to do the talent show."

"But—" Frankie began.

Maya shook her head. "It was *your* idea. I knew I'd be too scared."

Frankie bit her lip. Maya was right. Frankie had assumed they'd both wanted to do the talent show because they'd had so much fun performing for their parents. But they had never actually talked about it. Sometimes Frankie got so excited about things, she didn't slow down to think about what she was doing. "You're right," Frankie said. "I should have asked you first. I'm sorry for that, too."

Maya sniffled.

"You like doing magic, though, right?" Frankie asked.

"Sure," Maya said. "It's fun to do it for our parents. But other people are . . . different, I guess. It makes me feel all sick inside to see them watching me."

"Did you imagine them in their underwear?" Frankie asked.

Maya wrinkled her nose. "What?"

"That's what you're supposed to do when you're scared: imagine people in their under- wear," Frankie explained.

Maya wiggled out from under the beanbag. "That's really not something I want to do." Maya wiped tears away from her eyes with the back of her hand.

"I think it's supposed to make you feel more relaxed," Frankie said. "Like, sure, you're onstage, but they're in their underwear. But I guess that just feels weird." Frankie thought a little more. "Maybe we should meditate before the show, like how Ms. Pence taught us?" Ms. Pence was the school guidance counselor. Earlier that year she'd taught the third graders to meditate. Frankie wasn't very good at it— she had a hard time making her thoughts slow down. Maya, though, had liked it a lot.

"Maybe," Maya said. She looked down at her lap. "I thought I would be able to do the show. I really did. All last night I told myself it wouldn't be so bad. I said, 'It'll be just like in our living room.' But then this morning I felt sick. I've felt sick all day, actually. And then I got up onstage and—"

"You weren't going to barf, were you?"

"I felt like it," Maya admitted. "But it was

more like being frozen. I heard you talking. I heard my cue. But when I opened my mouth, nothing came out." She put her head in her hands. "You should probably find someone else to be your assistant."

"No," Frankie said.

"I bet Ravi would do it," Maya told her.

"No way," Frankie said. "You are my one and only assistant."

"Well, I don't know what to tell you, Frankie. This assistant has a serious case of stage fright."

Frankie stood up and put her hands on her hips. "You have a problem, Maya, and there has never been a problem that I can't solve. I am the Great Francesca."

"I don't think you know enough magic yet to fix this," Maya said.

"Fine," Frankie said. "But I have other talents."

"Ventriloquism?" Maya asked.

Frankie grinned. That would be hilarious, but there was no way she could learn how to make her voice come out of Maya's mouth in time for the talent show. "No," she said. "Invention. I am going to invent a solution to your problem! I am the world's greatest third-grade inventor, after all."

"If you say so," Maya said. She didn't look convinced. Her cheeks were blotchy and there were still tears in her eyes.

"I do! If you want to be in this show, then I will make it happen. I will beg Ms. Frost to let us be in the show, and I will invent a way for you to not be afraid."

Maya didn't say anything at first. She only chewed on her lower lip.

"You do want to be in the talent show with me, right?" Frankie asked.

Maya nodded. "Yes," she said. "More than anything."

"Then I will make it work!" Frankie declared. "I promise."

A promise is a serious thing, and Frankie didn't take it lightly. She knew she was going to have to come up with her best invention yet. She knew what she had to do first—find an expert. She needed to go see Mr. Winklesmith.

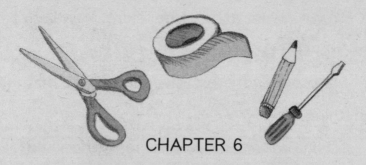

CHAPTER 6

The Jitterbugs

FRANKIE PULLED OPEN THE DOOR OF Wink's Magic and Games Emporium. It was her favorite place in the whole wide world. It smelled like circus popcorn and sawdust, and shone with a golden light.

While her mom stopped to browse through the new books, Frankie beelined for the back. She walked past the jigsaw puzzles in the spinning racks at the front of the store, past

the stacks of coloring books, past the stuffed animals. She even went past the building and science kits that always caught her eye. She stopped at the back counter, where Mr. Winklesmith kept the magic supplies.

Frankie knew that when you had a problem to solve, it was best to go to an expert, and no one knew more about magic than Mr. Winklesmith. He worked as a professional magician, performing at kids' birthday parties and town festivals. When he was younger, he had traveled across the country, performing.

No one was at the counter, so Frankie called out, "Mr. Winklesmith?"

He emerged from the back room through a curtain made of shiny plastic beads.

"Mademoiselle Sparks," he said. The stick of a lollipop stuck out of the corner of his mouth.

"I am in dire need of assistance," she said.

"Dire?" he asked.

"Serious," she said. "Major."

"I see," he replied, stroking his white goatee. "Dire problems call for Gobstoppers." He reached behind her ear and then held his fist in front of her nose. He opened one finger at a time to reveal a bright yellow Gobstopper.

Frankie took it from him, unwrapped it, and popped it into her mouth. It took up most of her cheek. "It's my assistant," she said. The words came out like underwater bubble-talk: *Ibs my abbibtan.* "She has a serious case of stage fright."

Mr. Winklesmith nodded. "I see," he said again. He scratched at his wrist, then began pulling scarf after scarf from his sleeve. Frankie knew that he did simple tricks like this to help him think, so she kept talking. She explained how Maya had gotten so nervous that she had dropped their props and scattered the cards all over the stage.

"That is a tough problem," he said. "Your friend Maya has the jitterbugs."

"The jitterbugs?"

"A case of the nerves. Finger feathers. It's happened to the best of us."

"Not to me," Frankie said.

"Never?"

Frankie frowned. She supposed her hands did shake a little when she needed to read in front of the class.

"I told her she should imagine everyone in their underwear," Frankie said.

"That just makes the performer *look* more confident. It doesn't stop the pitter-patter."

"What does?"

"Nothing," Mr. Winklesmith said.

"What? You mean it's hopeless?"

"Did I say it was hopeless?" he asked. "Do you know why people's hands shake when they're nervous?"

Frankie shook her head.

Mr. Winklesmith took his lollipop out of his mouth and placed it in a special dish on the counter, so Frankie knew he was about to get serious. "It's like this," he said. "Imagine your brain is like the captain of your body."

"The brain *is* the captain of the body."

Mr. Winklesmith raised an eyebrow at her, and Frankie knew she should zip it. "Hold out your hand," he told her. "And hold it still. Do not let it move at all."

Frankie held her hand above the counter. It was still and as flat as a plate. After a minute or so it gave a slight twitch. "Whoa!" she said. "How'd you do that? How'd you make my hand twitch?"

"I didn't," he told her. "All of your brain is

focused on keeping your hand still, and eventually your brain gets tired, and then it's like it sends a little message to your hand—not on purpose, but just because it's tired. And the muscles in your hand contract."

"Okay?"

"Now imagine you were trying to keep your hand still while I tossed tennis balls at you."

"It probably wouldn't go so well."

"Anxiety, being nervous, that's like someone popping up and bouncing balls at you when you're trying to concentrate. So your brain starts sending the twitch message over and over, and then your hand will start to shake."

"Huh," Frankie said. Because it was interesting. But then her stomach dropped. "So it's built into us?" she asked.

"Yes, that's right."

"Then it *is* hopeless," Frankie said, and slumped over onto the counter. She found herself face-to-face with a fake thumb, and even that couldn't cheer her up.

"Maybe stopping the jitterbugs themselves is hopeless, but that doesn't mean you and your assistant can't find a solution. You just need to know what problem you're solving."

Frankie lifted her head up. She knew that inventing started with identifying a problem. Her problem was that Maya's hands shook. She thought she needed to stop the shaking, but Mr. Winklesmith was telling her that wasn't possible. So what problem could she solve?

She thought about this question while Mr. Winklesmith sucked on his lollipop.

"If I can't stop her shaking, then I need to find a way that she can do the tricks even if she *is* shaking?"

"Precisely!" Mr. Winklesmith said, taking his lollipop out of his mouth and jutting it toward her face. "You need a work-around."

"Like what?"

Mr. Winklesmith picked up a piece of paper. He folded the paper over and over and then took a pair of scissors out of a cup on the counter. As he spoke, he made small snips in the paper. "Once, when I was a little boy, I was helping my father bring in wood for our fire. My arms were small, and I could only carry one log at a time. By the time I got a load of logs in, all the heat from the fire had escaped out the back door. So my father built me a log carrier, and then I could bring in five logs at a time. The house stayed warm, and everyone was happy. Especially the cat."

He stopped cutting and unfolded the paper. A paper house popped up, with smoke seeming to puff out of the chimney.

"Mr. Winklesmith, that is beautiful. But I have no idea what you are talking about."

"If she's dropping the cards, you need to find a way to help her hold on to them." He wiggled his fingers.

"But how can I do that?"

"You need to give her a hand!" Mr. Winklesmith laughed at his own joke.

"Mr. Winklesmith!"

"Sorry, Frankie," he giggled. "But that's the best I can do."

Frankie frowned, and then Mr. Winklesmith reached into the glass case and pulled out a purple feather. "It's on the house, Frankie."

Frankie's eyes widened. She couldn't believe Mr. Winklesmith was giving her an Incredible Feather. She could do all sorts of new tricks with it! But what good were new tricks if she still didn't have her assistant by her side?

"I'm sorry about your friend, Frankie, but you'll figure it out," he said. "You always do."

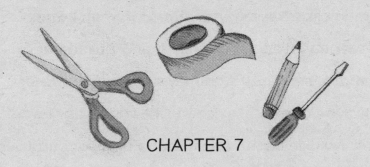

CHAPTER 7

Card Game

"IT'S TOO BAD YOU CAN'T BE IN THE talent show," Lila said to Maya the next morning. "Ms. Frost says that when we have rehearsal, we get to have pizza."

"With extra cheese!" Luke piped in.

"Oh," Maya said. "That sounds cool."

"I bet you would've been really good, too," Lila said. "Do you have a costume? I bet you could wear something fun if you were a magician's assistant. I would wear a mask over my eyes. Or a fancy hat. With feathers and glitter and everything. A black one or maybe purple."

Frankie had to admit that a black or purple mask with feathers and glitter sounded amazing, but she was too mad to give Lila a compliment. "Who says we aren't doing the talent show?" Frankie asked.

Lila looked at Frankie, then at Maya, then back at Frankie. "Your audition was kind of a disaster."

"Ms. Frost said we can be in the show," Frankie told them. She had gone and spoken to Ms. Frost just like she'd promised Maya. Frankie had explained that Maya was a little nervous, but that they'd keep practicing and would have it under control. To her friends in her class, though, she said, "We just didn't want to show you all our best tricks—right, Maya?"

"Um . . . ," Maya said.

Frankie puffed out her chest. "I mean, maybe we have a few very small problems to work out, but we'll get it. And our act will blow your mind."

"You're really going to do the show?" Lila asked Maya.

Maya looked over at Frankie. Her eyes were wide and she looked uncertain. Frankie gave her a nod. "I guess so," Maya said.

"We will be there," Frankie said. "Don't you worry!"

She grabbed Maya by the hand and pulled her over to the hermit-crab tank, where their class pet, Lenny, poked his head out of his shell and regarded them with mild interest.

"Did you solve it, Frankie?" Maya asked. "Did you come up with an idea to solve my problem?"

"Not yet," Frankie confessed. "I went to see Mr. Winklesmith, but I still don't have my great idea yet."

"What did he say?"

"He said I needed to find a way to help you hold the cards."

"That's not exactly helpful."

"I know," Frankie said.

Ravi, who was sitting at a table nearby, leaned his chair back. They were supposed to keep four legs of the chair on the floor at all times, but Ravi was a perpetual leaner. "You know," he said, "I get nervous sometimes too."

"You do?" Maya asked.

"Sure," he said. "At my first piano recital, I actually threw up—"

"Ravi!" Frankie said. "That's not helping."

Ravi shrugged and turned back to his worksheet.

Maya, though, asked, "And then what happened?"

"Nothing," he said. "I threw up in the trash can backstage, I put some gum in my mouth to make the taste go away—"

"Ew!" Frankie said.

"And then I went out and played. I figured if throwing up was the worst thing, then I could handle it."

"Throwing up is pretty awful," Maya said.

"It is," Ravi agreed. "But I could handle it. Just like you. You had a really bad audition, but so what? You're fine, right?"

"I guess," Maya said.

"I think I see what you're getting at," Frankie said. "You were really scared that a bad thing would happen, and then a bad thing *did* happen, and it was bad, but you were okay."

"Yeah," Ravi said. "Exactly. No matter what happens, Maya, you're going to be okay. I know it's hard, but that's what I remind myself when I go onstage."

Before they could talk about it any more, the door opened and their kindergarten buddies streamed in. Violet ran to Frankie and wrapped her arms around Frankie's waist. "Do you want to see a magic trick?" Violet asked.

"You bet I do," Frankie answered.

Violet held up a wooden coin. "Do you think I can make this coin disappear?"

"I do!" Frankie said.

"Me too," Maya agreed.

"You're supposed to say, 'That's impossible!'" Violet told them.

"Oh," Maya said. "Let's try again."

Violet nodded. "Do you think I can make this coin disappear?"

"No way!" Frankie said.

"That's impossible!" Maya said.

Violet held the coin up in her hand and showed both sides. She carefully placed it in her palm, then curled her palm into a fist. "Abracadabra!" she said. When she opened her fist, the coin was gone.

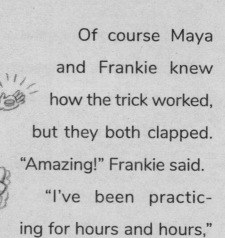

Of course Maya and Frankie knew how the trick worked, but they both clapped. "Amazing!" Frankie said.

"I've been practicing for hours and hours," Violet said.

"Maybe she should be your assistant," Maya said. Her smile faded into a frown.

"Really?" Violet asked.

Frankie shook her head. "Sorry, Violet. Maya is my one and only assistant. But you keep working on your tricks, and you'll be a magician in no time."

"Girls," Ms. Cupid said. "Let's settle down."

Frankie took Violet over to the floor cushions while Maya went with Toby to read books. "Do you want to read a story?" Frankie asked.

"I learned a new card game," Violet told her. "I brought my card holder." She waved the paper plate card holder at Frankie.

"Hey," Frankie said. "Let me see that."

Violet handed the card holder to Frankie. Frankie examined it closely. "Handle," she mumbled, looking at the clothespins. "Good and strong. Easy to hold on to." She turned it around. It was a really simple design. Two half circles made from paper plates were held together tightly so that the player could slide a card in and it wouldn't fall out. The holder would be perfect for tricks where the cards needed to be fanned out. For the tricks where the deck needed to be stacked up, though, the holder wouldn't work. The deck was too thick to fit.

"Frankie?" Violet asked.

"Huh?"

"You're talking like a robot. Did you turn into a robot?"

"No, I—"

"Because I think I could use a robot. Every unicorn princess from outer space could use a robot."

Frankie almost responded to that statement. She figured it was probably true that if there were unicorn princesses in outer space, they would have robots. But she was too focused on the card holder. The way it was designed wouldn't work for Maya and their card tricks, but it was making her wheels turn.

She could make her own special card holder, one just perfect for Maya the Magnificent.

"Frankie?" Violet asked again.

But she wasn't going to simply copy Violet's card holder. She was going to improve it.

"Are you okay?" Violet asked her.

"Yes," Frankie said. "I'm better than okay. You just helped me come up with my next great invention—and saved the talent show."

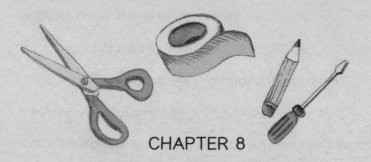

CHAPTER 8

Making the Hand

FRANKIE'S IDEA ITCHED INSIDE HER all day. When school was out, she burst through the doors and raced down the stairs past her waiting mom.

"It must be an invention day," she heard her mom say to one of the dads.

"Come on, Mom!" Frankie called over her shoulder. Her mom caught up with her, and Frankie immediately started talking. "It's a hand, Mom! Mr. Winklesmith was right. I need to give her a hand. A hand that can hold the cards even when she shakes, so that she can still do the card tricks."

When they got home, Frankie took the front steps of their house two at a time and didn't even stop in the kitchen for a snack. She went straight to her invention lab. The lab had been a closet, but she and her parents had cleaned it out to make her a work space. She had a small table and a pegboard full of tools. She had crates full of cardboard scraps, Lego bricks, wires, and more.

She rolled out her stool and sat down. During quiet time at school she had made several sketches, and now she laid the crumpled pages on her desk. The card holder Violet used was just two half circles held together tightly enough that the cards stayed in, but loosely enough for Violet to pull the cards out when she needed to play them. That was fine for some tricks, but Maya needed to be able to hold the whole deck of cards too. She needed a thumb.

Frankie looked at her supplies. Her design called for a handle and then something flat to hold the cards. She dug through her recycled-materials bin. She found lots of tubes: paper-towel tubes, toilet-paper tubes, wrapping-paper tubes. Any of those might work, but then what would she put the cards on? It needed to be flat and hard.

She stood up and balanced on one foot. Balancing helped her to concentrate.

A handle with a flat part. A handle with

a flat part. She repeated the words over and over in her head.

Then it came to her.

But what she needed wasn't in her invention lab. It was in the kitchen. She poked her head out of her lab. She could hear music coming from her mom's office, which meant her mom was hard at work too. Good.

Frankie walked softly in her sock feet into the kitchen. Next to the stove was a jar full of wooden spoons and whisks and other things her parents used while cooking. Right in the center she found what she needed: a spatula.

She took it out of the jar. She wasn't sure what her parents would think about her taking it. She figured that if she made the card holder, she could show it to them. And anyway, she had a lot of allowance saved up. She could buy them a new spatula. She was saving up to buy a robot that she could code, but sometimes inventors had invention emergencies. And this was definitely an emergency.

Next, she opened up the junk drawer and pulled out an old deck of cards. She would test out the design with old cards to see if there were any problems. She didn't want to ruin her magic deck.

The hard part was figuring out how to keep the cards in place. She wanted a bar that would snap back on top of the cards like a swinging door snapping shut. She found a clothespin and put that on the spatula. It clipped well, but it wouldn't open up enough to hold all the cards. Her first thought was that she could take the clothespin apart and put it back together, but that didn't work.

Back in her invention lab, she looked at her supplies. She balanced the cards on the spatula. It was a pretty narrow spatula, and the cards hung over the edge. "They need something to lean against," she said. Sometimes when she invented, she talked to herself. She'd once heard it was something many geniuses did.

She fished a scrap of cardboard out of the recycle bin. She placed it perpendicular to the spatula, the cardboard underneath the plastic. Using duct tape, she attached the two together.

Now it looked like she had a *T* on the end of her spatula. She folded up one edge of the cardboard like a wall. The cardboard made a base for the cards. The cards could sit on the spatula, and the cardboard would keep them from sliding off in that direction.

Next, she needed something to hold the cards down. The clothespin wouldn't work, but what if she could make something that pinched like a clothespin? She found a Popsicle stick— from a fudge pop, her favorite—and a rubber band. She cut a slit through the wall part of the cardboard and slid the Popsicle stick through. The Popsicle stick went across the cards and stuck out on both sides. It held the cards down, but not tightly. That was where the rubber band came in. She wrapped the rubber band around the Popsicle stick where it stuck out of the card-board wall. Then she tugged the rubber band down under the spatula and around to the other end of the stick. She looped the rubber band onto the other end of the Popsicle stick.

It was perfect! The cardboard kept the cards where they were supposed to be on the spat-ula while the Popsicle stick and the rubber band worked together to hold the cards snug against the spatula. When she took part of the deck out, the rubber bands pulled the Popsicle stick down and held the remaining cards tightly. She could even swing the card holder around and the cards didn't fall out.

She put her new invention down on the table. It worked perfectly, but she was a little disappointed when she looked at it. It looked

like a spatula with card-
board and a Popsicle
stick attached to it.
It didn't look magical or
special at all.

She frowned. But then
she thought about what
Lila had said about fancy
magician costumes. As
much as Frankie hated to
admit it, Lila was right. Magic
was all about the show, the glitz, the sparkle.
Luckily, Frankie had plenty of flair. She added
ribbons to the end of the spatula and covered
the handle in shimmery red fabric. "Ta-da!" she
announced. "I give you . . . the Great Card-ola!
A new magic device that every self-respecting

magician will want in her magic bag."

"Is that my spatula?"

Frankie turned around. Her mother stood in the doorway.

"It was the family spatula," Frankie said. "Now it's the Great Card-ola."

Her mom frowned. "Frankie," she said. "You can't just take the spatula."

"But look," Frankie said. She showed her mom how the Card-ola worked. "See? When Maya's onstage, she can still hold the cards, even if she shakes from nerves."

Her mom said, "You owe me a spatula." But she was smiling a little, so Frankie figured she wasn't in too much trouble. And anyway, she had saved the talent show. She could handle being in a little trouble for that.

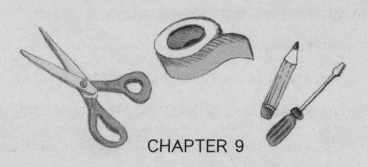

CHAPTER 9

The Show

FRANKIE GRINNED AT MAYA. MAYA TRIED to smile back, but she looked more like a bear showing her teeth.

They were backstage. Ravi was onstage, finishing up his comedy routine. His jokes had actually been funny, and people were practically rolling in the aisles laughing.

Maya's lips were moving, but Frankie

couldn't hear what she was saying. Frankie leaned in closer.

"I'm going to be fine. I'm going to be fine. I'm going to be fine," Maya whispered over and over.

"Are you sure you want to do this?" Frankie asked.

Maya didn't answer at first. She sank farther back, as if she wanted to disappear into the curtain. But then she whispered, "Yes."

Frankie grinned. "Good," she said.

Onstage, Ravi told a joke that made the audience groan. "Okay, okay," he said. "I've got one more for you. Knock, knock."

"Who's there?" the audience called back.

"Thank," he said.

"Thank who?" they replied.

"Thank you!" he said, and the audience started clapping.

When he had cleared the stage, Ms. Frost spoke into the microphone. "Up next we have the Great Francesca, Empress of Magic, and her marvelous assistant, Maya the Magnificent!"

"That's us!" Frankie exclaimed.

Frankie tugged her hat down on her head and grabbed her magic bag. Maya rolled their table out onto the stage. Their magic cabinet was already set up toward the back.

"Break a leg," Ravi told them. He didn't mean it for real. That was how performers wished each other luck. Frankie flashed him a thumbs-up sign.

Frankie placed her magic bag on the table

and began arranging the items inside while the crowd hushed. When everyone was quiet, she turned and faced the audience. She pressed her fingertips together as if she were concentrating very, very hard. Mr. Winklesmith had told her that was how you got the audience under your spell.

"Ladies and gentlemen," she said slowly. "Boys and girls. Prepare to be amazed. You are about to see feats of magic the likes of which you have never experienced before. You will be stupefied!"

She shook out her sleeves. Inside her sleeve was the long scarf she needed for the first trick. They had come up with a list of tricks for which Maya didn't have to handle too many props. They'd decided to do an easy one to start, to make sure Maya was comfortable.

"I am the Great Francesca, Empress of Magic. For my first trick, I will feed my assistant, Maya the Magnificent, this scarf." She shook a scarf in her left hand with a flourish. "And pull it from her ear. Maya, are you ready to eat this scarf?"

Maya smiled and gave one big nod.

Frankie and Maya stood face-to-face, profiles to the audience. "This scarf, I will have you all know, tastes like butterscotch ice cream, Maya's favorite," Frankie said. She started feeding a scarf into Maya's mouth. Really she was tucking it back into her hand, but she moved her other hand quickly, and Maya made her cheeks bigger and bigger.

Maya turned to face the audience. Her

eyes were wide, but that was okay. It kind of went along with the trick. She kept her hands tucked behind her back so that people couldn't see them shaking. She made a big swallowing motion, let the air out of her cheeks, and rubbed her belly. Some of the younger kids in the audience gasped. But they hadn't even seen the best part of the trick yet.

"Let me help get that out of you, Maya," Frankie said. She held her hands up by Maya's ear and appeared to pull out the scarf. She hesitated for a moment, and then pulled out another scarf. And another and another. The scarves littered the floor. The audience gasped and clapped. Finally she pulled out the last scarf and held it above her head. Frankie and Maya each gave a small bow.

The audience clapped wildly, making Maya grin at Frankie. It was a small grin, to be sure, but it was something.

They did a coin trick, and the disappearing-in-the-box trick—which, Frankie had to admit, had been a little better when Opus had snuck in with her.

Now it was time for the grand finale. The great card trick. Frankie looked at Maya. Maya gave her a thumbs-up. It wasn't strictly professional, but Frankie figured it was okay.

"We need a volunteer from the audience," Frankie said. A sea of hands shot up. Frankie called on Violet.

Frankie took out her card holder. "For this trick, we will use a device specially designed for this magic show. This is the world premiere of the Great Card-ola, and it is only with us, the Empress of Magic and Maya the Magnificent, that you will see this trick performed in this daring manner."

Something else Mr. Winklesmith had told her was that it was important to raise the drama.

Frankie pointed to the deck of cards on her magic table. "I need you to shuffle the deck," she said to Violet.

"I've been practicing so I can be a magician like you!" Violet said.

Frankie grinned and put on her blindfold.

Violet shuffled slowly and carefully. When she was finished, Maya said, "Now pick a card, any card, and show it to the audience."

Violet pulled one card from the deck and

held it up so that the audience could see it. Now came the tricky part—getting the cards into the Great Card-ola. Maya held the Great Card-ola by its handle. It shook only a little. "Please place your card on top of the deck," Maya instructed. "Now, to make sure we don't know where the card is in the deck, please split the deck and place the top half into the Great Card-ola."

Violet stuck out her tongue as she followed the directions.

"And now, carefully place the remaining half on top of the other cards, hiding your special card in the deck."

Frankie pulled off her blindfold just as Violet placed the second half of the deck onto the first half. Frankie was able to glimpse the card that would be right on top of Violet's. It was the seven of clubs.

"Now I, the Great Francesca, will reveal your card."

While Maya held out the Great Card-ola, Frankie pulled out the cards one at a time. She held each one up to her forehead and then dropped it to the floor. When she got the seven of clubs, she took a deep breath. Carefully she pulled out the next card. She held it to her forehead. Just like before, she closed her eyes, then suddenly opened them wide. "This!" she cried out. "This is your card!" She turned the card to the audience, and they all started clapping.

Frankie, Maya, and Violet bowed together. The curtain closed, and they quickly gathered up their props and cleared off so that Lila could start her tap routine.

When they got offstage, Ravi was waiting for them. He gave Maya a high five. "You did it!" he said.

"Thanks to you," Maya said. "I just kept telling myself that no matter what happened, I would be okay, because I have good friends

like you. I mean, I was still terrified, but remembering that did help a little"

She turned to Frankie and gave her a big hug. "Thanks, Frankie," Maya said. "You're the most amazing magician, and inventor, and friend who ever lived."

And that, Frankie thought, was even better than all the applause that still rang in her ears.

CHAPTER 10

Can I Have One?

MS. McLEWIS, WHO HAD BEEN FRANKIE'S kindergarten teacher, stopped her in the hall on Monday morning. "Nice job in the talent show!" she said.

Frankie beamed.

"Do you think you could make me one of those Great Card-olas?"

"Do you do magic?"

Ms. McLewis shook her head. "No, but I

think some of my students could use it. I like to play card games with them, but some of their hands are pretty little, and it's hard for them to hold the cards."

"Like Violet," Frankie said. "That's where I got the idea in the first place. She has a card holder that can hold cards for games like Go Fish."

"Exactly! But you made one that works for other games," Ms. McLewis said. "Usually they put a pile on the table but this is way more fun!"

"Are you talking about Frankie's Card-ola?" Ms. Frost asked, poking her head out of her first-grade classroom.

"It's pretty cool, isn't it?" Ms. McLewis said.

"It is," Frankie agreed.

"I have some ideas for morning circle where each kid picks a card, but we haven't been doing them because my kiddos drop the cards all the time. Their hands are too small to hold the deck in one hand and select a card with the other. But with the Great Card-ola, we could pass it around and choose cards. That's much easier than passing around a deck. Do you think you could make me one too?"

Frankie beamed. She had only been thinking about Maya when she'd invented the Card-ola, but now all these other people wanted to use it too. Just like whoever had invented the spatula in the first place had had no idea that someone would modify it for card tricks. Frankie thought it was pretty cool the way you could make an invention for one purpose but have other people find all sorts of other uses for it. "I will get right on it."

Frankie marched on down the hall to Ms. Cupid's room. She felt as puffed up as a balloon about to burst. She met Ravi on the way in. "Good job at the talent show," she said to him.

"Thanks. You too," he said.

"I know," she answered.

Ravi shook his head, but he was smiling. Then he said, "Hey, Frankie, did you hear about the magician who fell through the floor during his performance?"

A magician who fell through the floor? Was this another problem for her to solve?

"It's okay," Ravi said. "He was just going through a stage!"

Ravi laughed at his own joke. Frankie groaned, but she smiled, too. Maybe, she thought, her next invention would be a joke

meter that would help Ravi find the funniest
jokes. She wasn't quite sure how she would
make something like that, but she knew she
could figure it out. She always did, because
she was Frankie Sparks, the world's greatest
third-grade inventor.

The Design Process

Problem Identification

Brainstorm

Design

Test Retest

Share

Something Old into Something New

HAVE YOU EVER HEARD THE EXPRESSION "We don't need to reinvent the wheel"? It means that when we start a new project, we don't have to go back and redo work that's already been done. When Karl Benz was making the first car, he didn't need to invent wheels—they already existed! Instead he focused on creating an engine to power the vehicle.

When we think of inventors, we often think of people coming up with brand-new ideas. Ideas that are wild and original. Ideas that no one has seen before. Sometimes that happens, but a lot of times people use ideas that already exist, and modify or improve them to make something new. That's what Frankie did in this story.

When Frankie wanted to make a card holder for Maya, she used Violet's card holder as an example. Seeing it sparked an idea, a brainstorm. When Frankie realized she needed something with a handle, she didn't invent a new handle; she used one that already existed—the spatula! She combined these two ideas into one to design her Great Card-ola.

Frankie was only thinking about Maya when she invented her Great Card-ola, but her teachers thought of other uses for her invention, such as helping their students hold flash cards. That's what's great about designing—it never really ends. Ideas grow and change and are used and reused over and over again.

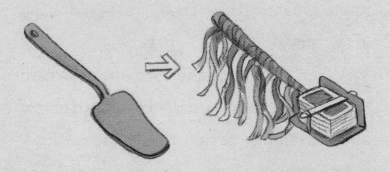

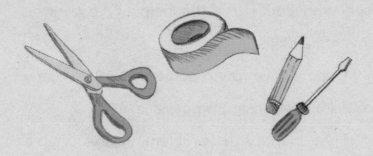

Your Turn to
Be the Inventor!

FRANKIE USED HER INVENTION SKILLS
to help Maya be in the talent show. Do you
have a friend or a family member who has a
problem that's getting in their way? Maybe
you have a little brother or sister who can't
reach their favorite cereal in the pantry. Or
maybe your teacher is always losing her
favorite dry-erase marker. Ask around and

see who could use the help of your great invention skills.

Once you've found someone, you're ready to follow the design process:

First, identify the problem. Interview your friend or family member to get as much information as you can about the problem. Ask questions such as "When does this problem bother you?" and "What have you tried in the past to solve the problem?"

Second, brainstorm. For this challenge, think about everyday objects you already have in your house or classroom that you could use to help solve the problem. Remember, there's no need to reinvent the wheel!

Next, design and build your solution.

Then it's time to test your design. Test it

yourself first and see if there are any areas that need improvement. When you think it's ready, bring it to your friend or family member and get feedback from them. Does it solve their problem? Keep redesigning and testing until you are both happy with the solution.

Finally, share your solution by giving it to the person. You can also share it with other friends, family members, or teachers. They will be excited to see your work!

Acknowledgments

Writing a book is its own special version of the design process, one that is made better through collaboration, so I have many people to thank:

Everyone at Aladdin for jumping on board with Frankie, especially editor Alyson Heller.

Illustrator Nadja Sarell for bringing Frankie to life so vibrantly.

Karen Sherman and Bara MacNeill for catching all the details.

My first reader, Jack Blakemore, who gave me honest feedback.

My character-naming helper, Matilda Blakemore. Frankie literally would not be Frankie without Matilda.

My agent, Sara Crowe, who always finds the best homes for my projects.

My family who supports me every step of the way.

And a very big, special thanks to my students and colleagues at Dyer Elementary in South Portland, Maine. You all inspire me every day!

Don't miss Frankie's next invention!

Sparkle Spa

Making friends one Sparkly nail at a time!

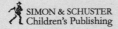